THOMAS & FRIENDS™

AS SEEN ON DVD!

START YOUR ENGINES!

Reds Against Blues!

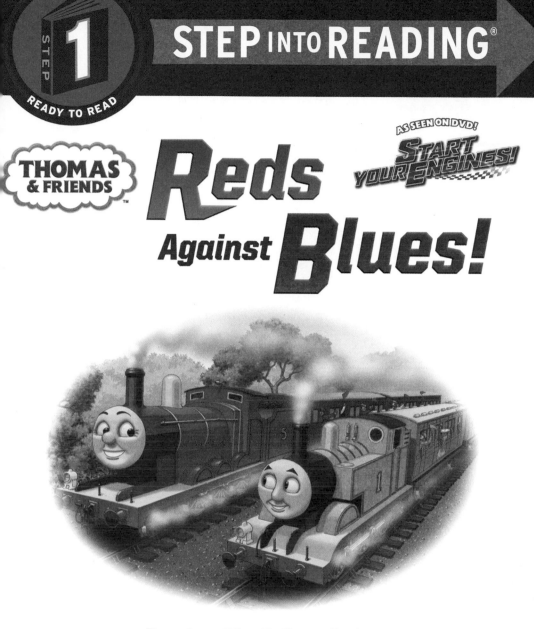

Based on The Railway Series
by The Reverend W Awdry

Illustrated by Richard Courtney

Random House 🏠 New York

James is red.

Dear Parents:

Congratulations! Your child is taking the first steps on an exciting journey. The destination? Independent reading!

STEP INTO READING® will help your child get there. The program offers five steps to reading success. Each step includes fun stories and colorful art or photographs. In addition to original fiction and books with favorite characters, there are Step into Reading Non-Fiction Readers, Phonics Readers and Boxed Sets, Sticker Readers, and Comic Readers—a complete literacy program with something to interest every child.

Learning to Read, Step by Step!

Ready to Read   Preschool–Kindergarten
• big type and easy words • rhyme and rhythm • picture clues
For children who know the alphabet and are eager to begin reading.

Reading with Help   Preschool–Grade 1
• basic vocabulary • short sentences • simple stories
For children who recognize familiar words and sound out new words with help.

Reading on Your Own   Grades 1–3
• engaging characters • easy-to-follow plots • popular topics
For children who are ready to read on their own.

Reading Paragraphs   Grades 2–3
• challenging vocabulary • short paragraphs • exciting stories
For newly independent readers who read simple sentences with confidence.

Ready for Chapters   Grades 2–4
• chapters • longer paragraphs • full-color art
For children who want to take the plunge into chapter books but still like colorful pictures.

STEP INTO READING® is designed to give every child a successful reading experience. The grade levels are only guides; children will progress through the steps at their own speed, developing confidence in their reading.

Remember, a lifetime love of reading starts with a single step!

Thomas the Tank Engine & Friends™

CREATED BY BRITT ALLCROFT

Based on The Railway Series by The Reverend W Awdry.
© 2016 Gullane (Thomas) LLC.
Thomas the Tank Engine & Friends and Thomas & Friends are trademarks of Gullane (Thomas)
Limited. Thomas the Tank Engine & Friends and Design is Reg. U.S. Pat. & Tm. Off.
© 2016 HIT Entertainment Limited.

Visit us on the Web!
StepIntoReading.com
randomhousekids.com
www.thomasandfriends.com

Educators and librarians, for a variety of teaching tools, visit us at RHTeachersLibrarians.com

ISBN 978-1-101-93284-1 (trade) — ISBN 978-1-101-93285-8 (lib. bdg.) —
ISBN 978-1-101-93286-5 (ebook)

Printed in the United States of America
10 9 8 7 6 5 4 3

Thomas is blue.

Sodor's soccer team
wears blue, too!

Sodor fans cheer
for Thomas.
They love blue!

Today is the big game!

James and Thomas
will pick up the fans.

The Sodor fans
wear blue.
They cheer for Thomas.

The other fans
wear red.
They cheer for James!

It is a race!

Reds against blues!

James cannot wait.

He wants to win.

James pulls away.

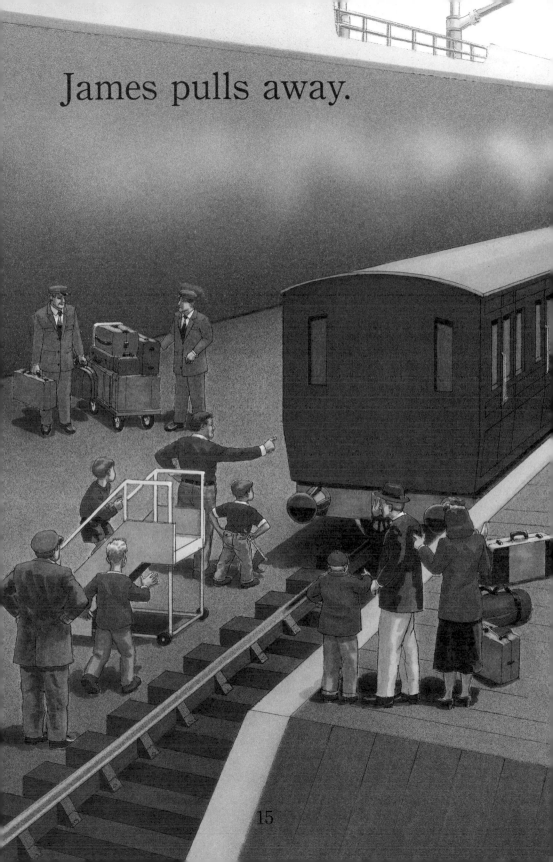

Thomas does not stop.

He wants to win, too!

He races past.

It is a tie.

What a race!

But where is

the soccer game?

James left the red team
at the station.

Thomas did not stop
for the referee.

Percy, the green engine,
saves the day.

Now the game
can start!

James and Thomas
get the yellow card.
Now they will work
for the same goal.

Goal!